The Wish And Other Short Stories

J. J. Robbins

Dedication

For all my friends and family that were my willing readers to make this possible. Especially my children, who have been patient with all my musings and late nights.

Acknowledgment

This work would not be possible without the time of my professors and fellow writers at Denver University and the amazing staff of Amazon Publishing that put in so much effort to make this what it is.

CONTENTS

About the Author

J.J. Robbins was raised in the deserts of Southern Arizona, but currently enjoys the open plains and majestic mountains of Colorado. She has a Bachelors in History and is currently working on her Master's in Creative Writing at Denver University. She loves to photograph nature along with her passion for reading and writing. She lives in a fun little house that was built in the 1890's that she shares with two of her four kids, a snake and according to her youngest, a resident ghost that got named Sir Cedrick the Third.

Page Blank Intentionally

The Wish

She was the first in many long years who actually saw him, he mournfully thought, as dandelion tops floated towards heaven.

The air filled with soft buzzing of bees and flies, and the occasional *whiff* from the Bull's nose. Off in the distance, the tinkle of a young girl's laughter broke the morning's tranquility. His ears twitched, but he did not move his head from his grazing. The laughter was distant, disembodied, and not worth his attention. The soft breeze smelled of earth and new growth. Yellow and white heads of dandelions bobbed up and down in rhythm like puffy hooded Russian Kalinka dancers. Above him, white wisps streaked across a bright blue sky. The early summer sun caused the morning dew to sparkle like diamonds in the light. He stood there in the sea of green, head down, eyes closed, nose buried deep in the sweetness of the fruits of the field. He remained there day in and day out. He was not unlike so many of his kind in appearance. The one brown spot against a jade and azure canvas.

Beyond the field, a wooden fence, gray and split with age, lined the boundary. On the other side, a yellow-haired girl with cherry blossom cheeks and freckles on her nose climbed the ancient barricade. Her hair, long and loose, whipped around her sunny face with the soft wind. Bright eyes looked up to the sky with wonder. The sound of clanging brought her attention back to her yard. The Bull watched her body grow smaller as she leaped off the fence and darted toward her home. The way her hair bounced behind her reminded him of the dance of flowers in the field. Something about the child pulled at his soul, pulled him hard enough to venture over to where she had been.

From his viewpoint her little farmhouse was as peaceful in appearance as the field. Small gardens lined the building's area outside. Farm tools and machinery dotted the dirt drive and around the small red barn. A tire swing swayed from one of the many tall trees that separated the two buildings. The breeze picked up once more; a wild array of white puffs from the dandelions like snow raced out before him. He could not understand why she bothered him so. He closed his eyes. Nothing at that house was any different today than any other day. He snorted out a heavy breath, leaned against the wood, and turned his head back toward the field.

He has always been there as far back as anyone could recall. He was the single solitary animal that never left. He knew that to mankind; he was a completely average-looking creature. Nothing about him made him an animal that any farmer or homesteader would covet after, so he was left alone. The field had been there as long as he had, as far as any human could remember anyway.

Below his hooves the dandelions sat crushed into the ground. His weight halted their playful dance. He stared down at the imprint they made in the mud, like a mosaic tile.

Such a small thing.

He shifted the bulk of his body off the side of the fence, his weight causing it to creak but not give. With deft lips, he lifted the flattened flowers from their prison in the mud, knowing they would upright themselves. From a short distance he continued his observations. The girl watched her father, yet for a precious brief moment, her eyes darted back to him.

Does she see me?!

The desire to stand up to his full height overtook him for a flash of an instant, yet the feeling vanished as quickly as it came.

Ah, no. No. Of course not. No one ever does. Only the "greener grass" on this side is seen, never I.

He saw in her eyes the look of a wild creature longing to be free.

If those souls only knew. If they knew what it was like here, in the pasture every day, every night. They see the flowers grow and die. They see the dandelions' heads lifted into the air, dancing with the zephyr. The barley and rye nodded their heavy-laden tops, beckoning. I, too, wish to dance in the wind. This ground may hold life and death, but for me, it is nothing but an eternity.

He watched her wander down the lane towards the next farm, where a golden-colored sheepdog barked excitedly. He heard the child's gleeful chatter upon the air currents. He felt in his heart something he had ignored for some time now. Something about her caused it to grow stronger. He swung his head from one side to the other, bleated a low *moo* and moved back to the other side of the field, where he continued to be present but not be seen.

He reminded himself that the field was all that mattered. This place was to be sweet and beautiful. Nothing marred its appearance of perfection. The Bull merely watched the world around him move from one state to the next. Only the visits from his Mistress would change the scenery.

As if the thought of her was a summons, he felt her arrival. He knew she'd be at the spring but felt no need to greet her yet. He would not yield to her call like a pup. He would choose the time of their meeting. The Bull felt he had satisfied himself with his decision, yet a hunger in his heart gnawed at him. He heard Her call. He chose to graze on. As the sun rose higher in the sky, he ignored the familiar and undesired feeling once more.

The afternoon sun had gotten warm. He slowly walked up the hill to the bubbling spring. Relief would be found there. He looked about expectantly for Her yellow cloak. His Mistress had been there, he knew. She had not waited for him this time.

The spring was icy cold. He gazed at his reflection, warped on the black surface. The dark surface gave the impression of great, unyielding depth; a deep abyss. He dipped his muzzle to the murky surface and pulled a long swallow. The chilled water spread through his body, cooling him from the heat, yet he felt as empty as before. He heard the child in the distance, the sound of laughter closer than it should have been. He slowly moved his head towards the sound but did not lift it. He knew the child was out there, drawn in by the field. A part of him hoped she would see him, even come close. He knew that no one ever would, not once their eyes truly saw. He snorted and watched the ground with the hope of actively ignoring the child.

He sensed it. It was there for a flash of a moment. He knew the child had seen it. He raised his head quickly from the spring. All was quiet. The child was near, much nearer than before. He heard her voice calling out to the sky. It sounded pleading, sad, and lonely. He felt a strange sensation in his gut, a flutter. The air picked up his hair, tousling it about his horns.

Snorting, the Bull turned to the direction he knew the girl to be. He could not see her but knew her location all the same. The gnawing grew tighter. Under his hooves, the ground was dry and hard. The heat was now heavy and oppressive. He moved over to the foliage for relief. It still felt damp against his foreleg. His movement knocked the seeds from various flora and fauna from their stems. A rush of fluff and petals rose upwards.

Why did You call her here, my Lady?

Her answer reverberated in his skull. For the first time in ages, he did not agree.

I do not wish for it, he pleaded, but Her answer remained firm. He released a low, long, sad call to the sky. The summer breeze carried it away. Her demand pulse in his mind. *As you desire, my Lady, it will be done.*

He heard the girl approaching quickly. The Bull lifted his head and turned toward her. She was a way's off but would close the distance rapidly. He snorted and pawed twice but remained where he was. He knew she'd forget why she ran in his direction in a moment, his Mistress always made it so. He felt he needed to make a show of perturbation at girl's presence anyway, but deep down, his heart leaped a little. At the speed she raced towards him, it would only be a moment before she would be right at him.

Her approach did not falter as he expected it to do; rather, she was focused on him fully. He watched the little girl approach. For a moment, a feeling of warmth filled his heart. As quickly as he felt this ray of hope, it left.

The breeze stirred up the white heads of dandelions, they whipped past his face. Their wild dance in the air went out toward the girl, mixing into the flowing strains of her hair. Up into the sky, the little white flowers lifted as stars into the sky. The dandelion tops gave up their life in a beautiful display to fuel the next generation.

It was time. He knew it. The field and his Lady had let him know it. He stood still; the child was getting close now, he knew what would come next, his heart ached.

***

Caisea watched her father from the kitchen window. He walked the path between the house and barn in a predictable pattern, like an old dog that patrolled his territory. She rested her chin on her arms in the windowsill, while she observed her father. She knew he would never let her out of his sight for too long. He was just like the neighbor's sheepdog, always watching over his flock. Caisea didn't mind too much, and she knew that her father meant well.

Upon the thought of the sheepdog, she giggled a little. Her father had the same soft golden-colored hair as the working dog. His eyes were equally puppy-like, especially when he wanted her to give him a kiss on the cheek, and she'd playfully refused. She slid from the window to wander outside, drawn towards the open space across the lane.

Standing on the bottom of the fence, Caisea hoisted herself up to the top. She shouted over her shoulder, "Papa? Who owns the field? I have never seen anyone out here."

"Hmm? Oh, that field," the farmer put down his tools for a moment. He looked out into the field, "I, uh, really don't know, actually," he stretched his blonde stubbled chin, "I am told it belongs to a woman that everyone has always called The Lady in Yellow."

"Have you ever seen her?"

He looked at her for a moment, and confusion crossed his face for the briefest of moments. Her voice seemed to go distant, and the question went foggy in his mind.

"Sorry, My Little Blossom, what were we talking about?" he said absently, redirecting his focus back onto the paint-peeled piece of machinery, her inquiry all but faded from his thoughts. With a playful roll of her eyes, the little girl bounced off the fence and skipped to her father. She paused just a moment as she watched him mumble to himself about the broken plow before she kissed his bent head.

"You are working too hard," she sighed.

He looked up at her small face. In her bright blue eyes, he saw her mother. His little girl was a gift, a blessing. He saw the spirit of his beloved wife grow within his daughter each passing year. Letting a pressed breath escape his lips, he tousled her hair before turning back to his project. She reached up and patted his cheek. Her touch felt like flower petals to him, sweet and soft and enchanting. She was his little Caisearbhán, his dandelion, just like her mother before her. It was at times like this where he felt his wife's absence the most. He cleared his throat, shook his head and looked out to the field. That place held both joy and sorrow for him.

"Stay out of trouble," he mumbled while fighting with a particularly stiff bolt.

Caisea looked over to the field with longing in her soul. She knew she shouldn't go into someone else's property without permission. She thought about returning to the fence to see if she could see this "Lady in Yellow." At least it would be something new or different.

The distant sound of barking pulled her attention from the invitation of the field to the Murphy's house and their old sheepdog. The neighbors usually didn't mind that she came over and played fetch for a while. She liked the old pup. He was gentle and kind to her. He never growled at her or nipped her ankles.

The Murphy's yard was plain and simple as far as a farm went. A few vegetable gardens like her house, but far fewer flowers. Caisea often teased the older woman while she did her chores. Her favorite thing to do was to startle her from behind her sheets while she hung them to dry. Some days, when Caisea was feeling particularly impish, she'd pull the items off the line and drape them over the fence of the field across the road, blaming pixies or fairies for the trouble.

Mrs. Murphy always had a wonderful baked treat for her before she'd skip back home. That morning, however, she noticed that neither the kind older lady nor her husband were home. Though not unusual, she was a little disappointed; she was feeling both mischievous and lonely. She settled for keeping the dog company.

The game of fetch and chase was fun. She enjoyed the freedom of running around. She laughed as the dog would anxiously wait for her to toss the stick, only to bring it back but not really let go until she gave chase. He'd drop it eventually. The breeze shifted. It felt nice. The afternoon sun had baked its way through her sundress. The movement of air was welcoming. She was tired of chasing the dog, and hot. Without thought or reason, her legs moved towards the fence. She dropped the stick by the front porch, letting the dog run off with it without her. The floral smell and still damp grass of the field seemed very inviting.

There was a pull of the dancing dandelions, of darting birds and the distant sound of a *Moo* that called to her. Thoughts about the mysterious lady that owned the field still tugged at her mind. Giggling to herself with the thought of possible mischief, she crawled under the wooden fence. The moment the damp grass touched her bare legs, an electric power of joy shot through her little body. She knew her father would not approve of her going into the field. She shrugged off any thoughts of his disapproval; besides, she just wanted to pick some dandelions and maybe see "The Lady", what harm could that cause?

She opened her arms wide to embrace the breeze, the sky and the field. She bounded out to the untouched ocean of grass. Within moments, the tall blades and wildflowers engulfed the blonde head within its leafy waves. Down the hill, she raced through the grass, spinning her arms wide, letting herself feel the world whirl around her.

"Mama! Can you see me?" Caisea shouted upwards to the clouds.

She stumbled forward, tripping over a large lump in the ground. She hit the ground hard, landing on her hands and knees. She saw a flash of white for a split second. Caisea sucked in the air, closing her eyes tight. When she opened her eyes, she felt disoriented; she was not in the same field. All around her, the grass was ash gray and wilted. Below her hands, blackened earth, rolling with strangely shaped lumps. It looked as if the world had turned black and white. In front of her face, the only color she saw was the bright yellow burst of the dandelion blossom.

"Papa!" she screamed.

In her panic, she rolled over to her back and covered her eyes. She heard nothing but the rustle of the grass. She peeked through her fingers. Confusion filled her mind, followed by a dull fogginess that happened after waking up from a dream. The world looked normal once more. Above her, the summer afternoon shone brightly. Her voice had been lost to the sky. Dandelions and wildflowers with their brilliant colors and perfumed petals filled her senses. Around her, nothing more than a picture-perfect field of green. Her mind and body relaxed.

"Why did I call for Papa, Mama?" she absently asked the clouds and sky.

She knew that no answer would come; it never did, but she liked to think her mother could hear her. However, today, she felt more alone than usual. She closed her eyes, letting the sounds of the field fill her mind. She heard the birds in the distance, a chorus of twitters. The soft rhythm of the cicadas and a distant clang of her father banging on the old plow. The sounds were in sharp contrast to the sounds of the pasture but it was comforting to her, knowing he was still there.

The smell of earth and manure reminded her of sitting out in the gardens at her own home with her father, talking to the sky in hopes her mother could hear them. The tops of grasses and wildflowers kissed her fair, freckled skin; it tickled. The warmth of the sun embraced her. It felt perfect. She could sense that life was all around her. It enveloped her. The world was simple here in this field, an oasis from all cares. Her loneliness melted into the ground. She closed her eyes, sending her thoughts heavenward; she wished to stay there forever.

She lay there on her back long enough that the sun moved from her face to her shoulder. She soaked in the sunlight, and the breeze; the serenity of it kept her calm and still. The wind picked up; it felt different than before. Something about the air called to her to sit up; it whipped at her hair, and she felt like her soul needed to get up and run free. The snowy pappus of the dandelions whirled around her face and raced up to the sky. They seemed to disappear within a passing cloud. For just a moment, she wished to meet her mother. To her left side, a short white puff ball sat sheltered from the lift of the winds. Caisearbhàn delicately plucked the milky stem and brought it to her lips. She whispered a child's wish into the delicate orb. A short breath later, her feathered hopes rose into the air, joining others from the field.

Rolling to her stomach, she gazed out onto the open pasture and spotted the lone Bull grazing on a small rise, seeing him for what seemed like the first time since being there. She couldn't figure out why she hadn't noticed him before. Up by the spring, she saw a flash of yellow; she sat still. It was only for a moment, but Caisea swore she saw the mysterious "Lady in Yellow" looking at her. She lay crouched, and her eyes gazed intently at the figure. The cloaked lady seemed to have vanished with the swirls of her dandelion tops.

Caisea stayed crouched and wound up like a box spring. She had an almost catlike appearance. The movement of the Bull by the water pulled her thoughts away from the mysterious Lady. She did not see how the Bull had gotten there so fast. She didn't think she had sat there watching that long.

As if her tense position had heightened her other senses, she noticed the area in greater detail. The green was less green, and the distances were not as far as she thought. The air smelled less sweet but still had the inviting scent of water. The sounds of the insects were louder and seemed to be calling out to her. The air felt thicker and something with an unsettling amount of legs crawled quickly over her bare toes.

Her eyes dropped down to the level of the ground, it was incredibly lumpy and uneven, not just where she tripped earlier either. It looked as though the ground was littered with yellow, gray, and white stones and branches. The tall grass hid this imperfection. She disregarded it as just the way the ground was, despite the fact it had never been tilled. The imperfections of the field cause Caisea to feel like it is more alive and wild, like her. The mischievous energy from earlier rose like a fountain within her. Playfully, she pulled herself tight, eyes fixed on her target. She needed to share in the wild energy she felt around her. With a burst of energy, she raced for the Bull with laughter that trailed behind her.

****

The spot where Caisea kissed her father's forehead still felt warm. He paused briefly to see where she had walked off to. He was relieved she had not gone into the field but rather to the neighbor's. No matter how often he reminded her that it was not polite to trespass, she seemed to be pulled to it. From down the dirt lane, he signaled to his daughter with a wave. She waved back with a large smile on her face, with obvious disregard for his voiceless beckoning call. He never cared for her carefree wandering but knew she would ignore any pleas to remain home. She was a free-spirited child, so curious about everything around her. Like her mother, she would follow her heart no matter where it led her; it always made him worried about her. She was everything to him, so he indulged her whims. He watched her safely walk into Mr. Murphy's yard. Their sheepdog met her with all the excitement of a young puppy.

She always had a way with animals.

The thought made him glance over the pasture across the lane. It felt ominous. He tried to ignore the worry in his gut and threw himself back into his work. Mr. Murphy would need him to tend to his fields that fall, and his machinery kept breaking down.

The plow took far longer than he had hoped. The day had waned on to noon. Looking up from his repairs, he noticed his daughter was no longer playing down the lane. He looked down in both directions, and he didn't see her. He shook his head. He knew he worried more than he should.

He forced himself to return to his oil can, tools, and out-of-date plow. She was always bounding after one thing or another, a child full of wonder and harmless mischief. Deep down, he envied her freedom and innocence. With a smirk, he paused. His wife would have said something about him being silly for envying a child for being a child. Grateful that the breeze picked up once more to cool his brow, he looked out over the field across the way. He could smell the sweet and primal scent of flowers and grasses mixed with damp earth. Taking a reassuring breath, convinced himself that she wasn't far and would return by sunset as she always did. He refocused himself on the task at hand. His wife probably would have scolded him for being too protective of Caisea.

The sun had dipped past its zenith. As usual, he lost track of time while he worked. He wiped his hands clean of the oil and rust. It was finally finished. He pulled the plow back to the barn, noting the unsettling quiet. He walked into the house. He guessed that his daughter was probably still over at the Murphy's. A quick survey affirmed his assumption. Still, he knew he would feel better checking up on her.

As he strode out the kitchen door, a flash from the table caught his eye. Propped up against the table and window stood a picture frame. It was of his wife dancing in the field across the way in a pastel colored summer dress with dandelions embroidered along the edges. Her arms were open wide, eyes closed, face tilted upwards. A blissful smile crossed her freckled face. Her white-gold hair was fanned out from her body. It was his favorite picture; he took it the day they discovered that she was pregnant. Caisea must have been looking at it over breakfast.

He felt a heaviness upon his heart, "I wish you got to see her face, my love. Our Little Blossom is as wild and free as you were before..." he felt the warmth of a tear roll down his cheek. He had forgotten the draw of that place. It was in that field where he and his wife had snuck in and picked dandelions like children and made wishes on their snowy tops when they were newlyweds. Later, she told him that she had made a wish to have a little girl. When she got pregnant, she swore that her wish had come true.

That day she knew she was having a girl was also the last day she danced. From the moment she walked back home from the photo being taken, she deteriorated while the child within her grew. She never cursed or felt bitter about her health. She always smiled through it all, especially when he walked into the room.

He recalled how she would muse to herself that she walked into the pasture that day because it was like it was the first time she had ever seen it for what it was. She said it was Paradise. She told him, as she lay on the bed looking out the window, that the field was how she pictured heaven to be. He used to gaze out over the road to watch the grass wave, and it calmed him to think it might be where his beloved wife could be walking. He never could bring himself to enter it, though he did try. For some reason, every time he headed over, he would just turn around and come back home. Memories were bittersweet, he reminded himself. Leaving the photograph on the table, he walked out the kitchen door and down the road to Murphy's farm, where he'd probably find his daughter chasing an old sheepdog or eating sweets.

On his way to their house, he smiled to himself, and he felt foolish for his earlier feelings of disaster. The dust in the air mingled with wildflowers, and it had a delightful wild smell. He decided that it really was a peaceful day. He paused by the fence of the field for a moment. At his feet, a dandelion with two flowers peeked out from the boundary onto the road. A bright yellow disc is just shorter than a white orb. He picked up the orb and spun it between his fingers. He felt his heart ache; he wished his little girl could have known her mother. With a trace of child-like hope, he released the little seeds up into the air. He watched them float out towards the top of the field and towards the spring until he couldn't see them any longer.

He walked up the three wooden steps to the large Victorian-style porch, his passage blocked by the large yellow mass of fur. The sheepdog's head remained between his forelegs, but his ears perked up, and his tail thumped the wooden platform; it resonated with a hollow echo. Looking around, he failed to see his daughter anywhere around the yard. Upon approaching the back door that led to the kitchen, Mrs. Murphy swung it open before he could knock. His face was assaulted with the smell of freshly baked bread.

"Is Caisea around?"

A worried crease formed on the aged woman's forehead, "Sorry, I haven't seen her today. But we haven't been home until recently."

"Thank you," his voice was quiet.

"Don't worry, dear; I am sure she's around."

"I am sure. Thank you again, Mrs. Murphy."

He walked away from the house, his feet moving faster as he felt a deep, gut-wrenching fear pull him to a run.

"CAISEA!"

His feet pushed him harder down the dirt lane. He glanced at the field, his mind dismissed it quickly, like it was never there. He ran towards town with a prayer that she'd be there. His voice lifted to the air, mingled with a flurry of downy, white dandelion fluff.

***

He stood still; she was getting close now, he knew what would come next, his heart ached. As the young girl drew near, her face morphed from a bright smile to wide eyes and an open mouth. Her whole body tensed up, and it wanted to recoil away. Her momentum did not allow her to stop or turn. It was only moments before she reached within two arms' lengths of the creature.

The grass parted; Caisea blinked. All the color of the world had drained away, dripping away like paint in the rain. The field was hard, dry, and without life. All around, the wind blew away sand from the lumps on the ground that revealed skulls, hands and leg bones that were underneath. Her voice was caught in her throat as she saw it all. The scream never left her lips. The Bull was no longer fat and tawny brown. His skin pulled tight around an emaciated frame. He stared at her with eyes that glowed dark purple, and a mouth full of red-stained fangs. What stood before her was a demon with only the form of a bull. She was the first of many who saw him, the real him.

The movement was fast for such a large animal. In seconds, the two met. The sudden movement stunned her; she felt wet and hot. Her heart pounded. A tearing sound and a sharp pain blinded her to all else. The wet, sharp pain radiated from everywhere. The scream sought to escape from parted lips never came. What did was the sounds of bubbling water. She heard no other sounds, only the muted *thud* of something large hitting the ground. Above her, the face of a fanged bull-like creature looked down on her. Strangely, something about his eyes calmed her panicked soul. A look often she saw in her father and knew.

Sorrow. Loneliness.

Her eyes felt heavy, and a welcomed sense of sleepiness spread through her. The pain had vanished; just a dull, slow throb in her throat remained. Above her, a kind face hidden in a sunny cloak smiled at her.

The Bull watched his Mistress do her work with forced detachment. The Lady in Yellow stood over the small child; she gently placed the small broken hand into her own. She looked over at her Bull with a sad, apologetic smile upon her lips and vanished. In her place, an outline of bright white feathered seeds created a silhouette of her figure.

As the darkness closed around Caisea, a soft voice called out to her tenderly, "Hello, my Little Blossom."

Hello   *Mama.*

The sun continued its journey across the sky, reaching towards the horizon of dusk. The breeze disturbed the stillness, waking the insects and birds into their usual activity. The Bull watched the bloodied lips of the child part into a soft smile. The cherry color drained from her cheeks to the pool of red that was oozing around his hooves. A dandelion, once bright as the summer sun, now looked more like rust and drooped with the weight of her blood. Across the field, he heard the desperate calls of the father for his child. The fog of forgetfulness clouded his mind. That was the way of things in that place.

Maybe this time, he pondered, it was he who had called the child. Over the breeze, a call to the heart of those who wished. He knew she'd never be found, just like every other that lay under his hooves. He knew her father would look for the child for days, maybe even years, never once thinking she'd be in the field. It was his and his Lady's eternal duty to make it so. Only those called could walk his field, could step in and feel the bliss and wonder of "Paradise". All others would see what they wanted to see. People would look in awe, but why they looked away would slide away from their minds like a sweet, lost memory. The apparent perfection of his field inspired literature and art and made dreams. Those who were called there eventually saw the field, and some even saw him. All, always, would see Her, eventually.

He pondered on the little life draining into the soil. Her scarlet-soaked body would vanish into the world, just like every other. Her summer dress, now browning at the edges as blood dried, fluttered in the breeze, would rot away. Her flowing hair, like the clouds above, would blow off her rotting skull like the tops of dandelions. How short this life was. Much like the buzzing insects and the flowers around him. She had bloomed brightly, danced in the sun, and found a wish fulfilled.

Below him, the small broken body lay sprawled out on top of centuries of bones, her face oddly peaceful. She was the first in many, many years that actually saw him. The gnawing inside him returned deeper than before. Solitary in the field once more, to not be seen, to carry the secrets of the dandelions once more to his Mistress. He wished like so many others on the soft down of the dandelions but knew they'd go unanswered. Shaking himself off, he moved away from the discolored grass but cast a sad yet grateful glance at the child. She had seen him, and he had a purpose.

I am The Keeper of Wishes.

The Face of Our Demons

She could still hear the beast hunting her, its guttural growl and unearthly howl at the moon. The urgent thought spurred her forward. No matter how far she ran, its presence echoed around her, always sounding like it was just behind her. The sound of her feet hitting the ground seemed impossibly loud. Her heart pounded in her ears, but it did not drown out the beast's voice. Dried twigs and sticks like skeletal hands grasped at her feet. They pulled at the bottom of her skirt, tore at the hem, and caused her to pitch forward. She couldn't stop herself from falling. Tears raced down her cheeks as she pulled at her skirt, now a tattered and tangled mess in the dried-up undergrowth. Around her, the air grew colder, darker, and heavier. The sound of something large crashing through the woods drew ever closer.

"No. Not yet," she urgently whispered into the darkness.

Liz felt horror build up inside her. Her sharp breaths pulled in the painful, cold night air as she ripped away her dress, forcing herself up and forward once more.

The creature sounded closer than before. Everything around her seemed to grab at her, slowing her escape. Disturbed birds rushed upwards to the sky. Their black shapes covered the moonlight before landing somewhere else in the boney embrace of the canopy. The sound of their wings had momentarily drowned out all sound, only to be followed by an eerie silence. She knew it had to be close, or maybe it just watched and waited. Her mind raced. The only sound she could hear was her panicked breath. Her eyes darted from every shadow, and her skin prickled each time there was movement in the woods. Her heart would not accept what she witnessed when the moon rose only hours ago, yet she could not deny what she saw.

Her legs pushed her forward. She dared not look behind herself; the vision of its monstrous face and long fangs was still fresh in her mind. The terror of it served as the energy to spur her forward. Everything she knew had shifted, changed, and morphed. Trees that once were a welcomed sight twisted and groaned above her like a cage that closed her in. Darkness cast itself over every bush, stone, and tree. She had never seen it like this before. Somehow, the vibrant life of the woods had been leached away by the darkness and shone ethereal in the moonlight. The woods she called home had been replaced by some kind of nightmarish imitation. She chose a direction with the least resistance, any direction that did not have the boney hands clawing at her from the ground or could hide a large creature in the undergrowth.

In the distance behind her, a howl broke the silence. She felt a sudden surge of energy fill her weary legs. Mercury himself would have been impressed with her flight in the dark woods. Ahead, a large shadow loomed. She forced herself towards it. Anything was preferable compared to that which was behind her. As she drew near, the shadow took the form of a hut or small cottage. It didn't matter to Liz what it was or if anyone lived there as long as she could hide from the beast. The door gave away easily. She reached out blindly to find anything to block the entry. A small, worn table became her blockade, albeit a poor one. It was aged, termite-eaten, and probably a side table, given its diminutive size. Liz did not care. She shoved her back up against both the table and door. She pulled her knees up to her chest, dropped her head between them, and quietly sobbed. Her mind wandered to that fateful encounter when she saw it happen. She pounded her fists on the floor as she wept. The memories flashed as tears soaked into her skirt. It couldn't be real; what she witnessed could not be real. She desperately wanted what she saw to be nothing more than some horrible trick of her imagination. It was a plea, a prayer, lifted up to an empty room and cobwebbed ceiling.

The shaking sobs had ebbed to sniffling. She felt her heart slow down and took several calming breaths, deciding it was safe enough to take a look around the room. The smell of dust, rotted wood, and florals was strong and prevalent. However, underneath, a familiar and comforting scent lingered – the sweet, woodsy smell of whisky and oak. It reminded her of the Father she knew before that night. The wildness and strangeness of the room melted into a somber place of vague familiarity. Furniture became solid, recognizable forms rather than monstrous shapes in the dark. Slowly, she got up, noticing that whoever lived there hadn't been present for a very long time.

Despite its deserted appearance, something about the place had a calming effect.

Dried flowers on the mantle recalled images of her mother placing similar bunches around her home before she had become too weak to walk. Curious, she picked one up. It was old but not as old as she expected; the flowers still had a little give to their stems. The soft aroma of lavender mixed with the heavy, sweet, earthy smell of garlic blooms pulled her into a comfortable sense of home and normality. There was another floral aroma in the mix she couldn't place right away. It had a deep wintergreen smell that was mixed with layers of sassafras and licorice. It was oddly familiar. Wolfsbane, she thought, it had to be. Liz shook her head. Of all the places she could find refuge from that monster outside, it would be inside a hut that could have been a mirror image of her own. Absently, she dropped the flower bunch into the canvas bag that, mercifully, was still slung over her shoulder. Uprighting a stool, she leaned against the fireplace. She resisted the urge to stoke up a fire against the cold and darkness and allowed the chill of the night to seep into her body. Fatigue set in; Liz closed her eyes with her arms wrapped around her body, hugging the bag closer.

She could feel the weight of sleep. Her body sagged heavily against the hearth, the welcomed relief of rest beckoning to her as she floated in the vacant expanse of her mind. She felt both heavy and weightless at once. No images, just the blackness of deep sleep. Somewhere in the emptiness of sleep, she heard the faint voice of her Father. His constant goodbyes echoed in her memory. A solitary tear rolled down Liz's dirty cheek, but it did not wake her.

Silence filled her mind once more. Liz shifted, and the sudden loss of balance shocked her to consciousness, nearly knocking herself off the stool. She felt disoriented. Nothing looked right. It was still dark, and the space around her was both familiar and strange. The smell of dust and age pulled her into the present. As the events of the evening came back, so did the memory of the terror that brought her there.

"This has not gone as I had planned," she looked around her, "I should not have gone out after dark. Father warned us never to leave our cabin at night.

Now… now, I know why." Liz felt the lump reform in her throat again. "How is this nightmare real?"

As if her question was a summons, the stillness outside was interrupted by the sounds of footsteps. Liz rolled from her stool and back against the table and door. She pulled herself tight like a ball, hoping the creature with her Father's eyes would not see her.

"Lizzy?" a husky voice called out from the other side of the door, "Elizabeth, open the door. It will be safe for now," he said quietly.

Liz shook her head, her voice shaky, "Go away, you are not him," she felt her voice catch on her words, "You are not my Father! You are a Monster!" Liz felt the table bump forward a bit like something had pushed up against the door.

"Don't say that. Please, it's me, I promise."

"NO! GO AWAY!"

She tensed up and held her breath, but the door nor the table moved again. Liz stood up away from her blockade and leaned against the door, her ear pressed against the splintered wood. She couldn't tell if he was still outside. She felt a heat building up from her chest.

She pressed her forehead against the door, and salty tears of pent-up emotions raced down her cheeks.

"You ran out on us! Again and again! Mother is really sick this time, and I don't know what to do! What will happen to her? What will happen to me?" she cried, a hard, deep cry.

She wasn't sure when she moved from the door and he had pushed it open. She had sobbed so hard, letting the anger of his absence and her fear spill out with each tear that she had blacked out. He sat on the floor next to her, stroking her hair. His large hands, covered in dirt, scratches, and scars, had a gentleness about them. He looked down at his daughter. It was not a vision he had ever imagined he'd see. Her dress was so torn it appeared she had on rags. There was a mass of bramble tangled in her hair, and the dirt and debris that covered her from head to toe made her appear as lost as he knew she must have felt.

"I am sorry, my little Lizzy," he whispered after a quiet moment and got up. The movement caused Liz to awaken and sit up. She wiped her face with the back of her hand, causing a dark smudge across her cheek. She was relieved to see the familiar form of her Father.

His tall, broad figure strode across the room, then stopped suddenly, silhouetted by the window. Like her, his clothing looked torn and dirty. He kept running his hands through his disarranged hair. She watched silently as he kept moving towards different parts of the room, only to turn away like he found something repulsive. His usual confident gait was replaced by nervous pacing. He kept walking from the fireplace to a closet door by the back wall, and his face kept turning to the window behind her. Liz had not noticed earlier how the clouds obscured the moon. She watched as they raced across the sky, making the moon visible again.

Her Father's movements became more aggravated. He moved his head back and forth in an animal-like manner. His behavior and disheveled appearance suddenly made Liz more guarded. She slowly got up and touched his arm. He recoiled from the touch and swung his head around, and there was a predatory look in his eyes that softened immediately when they met hers. Liz realized he had forgotten she was there.

"Liz, you need to get out, now," his voice, now firm, demanded obedience. She looked at her Father and noticed something she had never seen in him before; fear and desperation. She nodded, picked up her bag, walked out without a word, and closed the door behind her.

Outside, the wild woods appeared less frightening. The atmosphere was quiet; a light breeze shifted through the pines, making them sound a bit like rushing water. She leaned against the door, tired. Behind the flimsy wood, she heard something heavy being dragged across the floor. There was a metal clang, then a click followed by a second clang. Confusion and curiosity filled her mind. The desire to open the door and look was strong, but she knew that would be a deadly mistake. As quietly as she could, she walked to the side with the window. She leaned close to the wall and rolled her head enough to peek in but not be seen. She knew what would happen, as she saw it earlier that night in the hills behind the house. When she saw her Father twist and deform from the man she knew, to something truly terrifying.

What she didn't expect was what she saw inside the cottage.

Inside, her Father had manacles around each arm. They were thick iron attached to heavy chains that led to a pulled-up floorboard. Underneath were a set of iron loops affixed to a stone. As the moonlight passed from behind the clouds, the pale beams landed on his slumped form. He sank to his knees, and his head drooped as the skin began to peel away from his bare back like a snake. From underneath, dark, tawny fur bristled out. The gentle hands that had held her numerous times curled inward with pain. Slowly, he stretched them out as they elongated and became lean and muscular. Black claws grew from each finger where his nails once were. His lean form grew broad, and his legs buckled underneath him; she could sense his agony as they twisted into powerful hunches of a canine. His head shot up, and she saw the tears that ran down his face as it contorted from the kindly face of her Father to the hideous muzzle of a very large wolf. His voice raised to the sky as he screamed, then morphed into a blood-curdling howl. As the howl died into the night, what stood shackled to the floor had no trace of a man left.

The large creature breathed heavily; its head swung from side to side as it sniffed the air. The wind picked up slightly, sending her scent into the cottage. It snapped its head in her direction. Liz froze. The creature moved its body so fast towards the window she couldn't respond. All she could do was scream. This sudden rush towards her caused her to fall over backward. She hit the ground hard. The sting on her backside felt especially sharp from the cold ground. When she fell, she swore she heard a heavy thud from inside.

Liz sat motionless. She squeezed her eyes shut and covered her ears in hopes that she could disappear altogether. She knew that she should return home, but her fear proved too great. Her mind jumped through images of what she had seen that night. She imagined seeing the great beast bursting through the door and devouring her. She recalled back to her escape into the woods when the predatory eyes fell on her behind the house. She saw his eyes as they filled with tears as he struggled to fight the demon within himself.

The breeze moved stray hair across her face, tickling her nose. She opened her eyes, dropped her hands to her lap, and strained to hear anything. When she heard nothing, she mentally berated herself. Her Father was also in there. He was just as lost and scared as she was. She got up and stared at the door. She took a few steps forward while her mind went over what she was to do next. She looked at her surroundings. It was strange to see the woods at night. Their shapes, so foreign hours ago, looked familiar once more. There was serenity there in the moonlight. The branches that reached out like bony figures were nothing more than dried saplings. The air filled with the smells of damp earth, oak, and flowers. The night was beautiful. In the cottage, she could hear the pacing of something big and heavy. Something inside of her burned, like a fire in the pit of her stomach. It wasn't like before when she was so angry, but something new. She shouldered her bag and pushed open the door.

The moment she entered, she saw the huge beast. When she passed over the threshold, it lunged at her but was pulled back by the length of the chains. The growls were low and threatening. He easily stood taller than her Father had. He looked like a wolf but far larger and more muscular, and there was an unsettling human likeness in the face and eyes. The deep brown eyes were her Father's. The same eyes she had seen earlier that evening in the hills. However, this time, behind the feral animal, she saw his gentleness, his kindness, and something else. His fear. Steeling herself, she walked in closer. She kept eye contact with the werewolf; he did not lunge again but followed her movement with a guttural growl of warning.

Liz slipped her hand slowly into her canvas bag and pulled out the flower bunch. She held it out in front of her like a saber.

"I now know why Mother had these bunches all over the house," she spoke with a quiet courage she really did not feel. The werewolf recoiled from the bouquet. As Liz looked around the cottage, she noticed that the flowers were not randomly placed but covered every possible exit except the door. Liz kept eye contact while she spoke, knowing that as she talked out loud, it was more for her benefit than it was for calming down the werewolf.

"You told me once that to overcome fear, sometimes you have to face it alone. I cannot speak for you, but I am tired of being afraid. It's exhausting,"

Liz tried to act as casual as she hoped she sounded, "I suppose it is not such a bad little place, really. Kind of reminds me of home. I mean, like if we forgot to clean it. Or decorated it. And everything in it was old. And you never fixed things."

The creature responded only with throaty growls. Liz surveyed the room as she took care to keep it just out of reach. Little things she had not noticed before became more apparent. The rotting wood was deeply scored by claws, and the familiar scent of her Father lingered due to his monthly self-confinement as he battled this demon monster alone. Her emotions felt like a tangle of ropes that she couldn't find the ends of. There was sadness, confusion, and fear still inside of her that mixed with a powerful feeling of gratitude. A mixture that felt unnatural to her. Liz walked over to her stool. All the while, she kept the flowers out in front of her to ward off the beast. She continued to keep eye contact with him while she carefully sat down. She watched as he paced; his eyes never left the flowers.

"I am sorry I called you a monster."

The beast stopped pacing and stared up at her. Liz lowered the flowers a bit; she watched him follow the bouquet with his eyes.

"You're not going to lunge at me again, are you?" Liz shifted and watched. The growling had stopped. He had backed away somewhat but maintained an aggressive stance while watching her and the flowers. Liz smiled weakly; she felt that she was beginning to understand a little bit.

"Father, if you can hear me, I am sorry. I was just so mad at you, and I'm scared. What if I can't take care of everyone?" Liz felt the warmth spread from her stomach into her limbs, "I am just so tired. I am afraid of being left alone. I am afraid that I can't take care of everyone. I can't do this alone, Papa!"

With her confession, she had dropped the flowers. The wolf leaped out at her, his mouth wide. With her last words still on her lips, fangs made contact with her arm, and she instinctively rose up against his advance. However, something stopped the creature before he broke her skin. Liz looked at the face of the monster, her breaths quick and short. There in his eyes, she saw him, her Father. The werewolf moved away from her arm, padded over to the cold hearth, and laid down like a house pet. Liz remained frozen. She glanced at her arm; not even a scratch had been made. Her mind whirled with mixed emotions and complete bafflement at what had just occurred. She quickly tucked her arm close to her body and thrust out the flowers. She remained in that tense position until her body began to ache.

Sleep had escaped her. Through the long night, she watched the mass of fur as it appeared to sleep by the empty fire. Her mind jumped from one thought to another. What stopped him from biting her; he had all intentions of attacking her before. What stopped him right then? Why had she stayed there and not run home? What would she do now that she knew her Father's terrible truth? The swirl of thoughts and emotions within her grew as the night progressed. Her Father had faced all of this alone. How long had he endured this curse, she wondered. She had so many questions. Questions that would have to wait until morning. If morning would ever come.

A gentle touch on her shoulder woke Liz. She blinked, not recalling that she had drifted off to sleep.

She looked around; the massive beast was gone. The flowers were in her lap, and her arm was still tucked in close to her body. She looked up to see her Father. He had a dusty blanket wrapped around his body. He looked like he had aged. Pain and guilt were written across his face, but a look of gratitude was also there.

"Hello, Lizzy," he rubbed the back of his neck uncomfortably, "I don't know what to say. I guess you probably will be afrai-"

Liz wrapped her arms around him and pulled him tight into her embrace, cutting off his sentence. He slowly lifted his arms around her. He pulled her in close and whispered, "You know, you haven't called me Papa since you were very small."

Liz pulled away, "You actually heard me?"

He nodded, "First time that has happened to me. I usually am lost in a dark sea when I change. But somehow, you found a way to reach me. That was both brave and very dangerous."

"I know. I don't understand it either. I wanted to run, but I saw how lonely and scared you were, and I couldn't. I just couldn't," Liz took in her Father's face.

She saw those same deep brown eyes. This time, she saw something very different than before; behind his gentleness, she still could see the wildness of the feral beast. She understood then that his battle was every day. That the warmth he had was born out of his pain and fear. Her Father motioned for her to sit.

"Are you alright? It didn't," he wouldn't look at her face, "I didn't hurt you, did I?"

Liz gently lifted her strong Father's face to look at her. He felt fragile, "It tried, but you stopped the beast, Papa."

He stared at his daughter, and she showed no sign of repulsion towards him. He felt the warmth of her hands on his face and the wetness of tears that he did not realize he was shedding. He pulled her in closer. Liz gripped him hard. She felt like she could stay protected in his arms forever.

"My brave little Lizzy."

She pulled herself out of his embrace. She looked at her feet while she shuffled them, "I am not sure if I am brave. I am still afraid of it. Although, when you had control, you looked like a really big hunting dog all curled up by the hearth."

He nodded, unsure what to say. Liz picked up her bag and returned the flowers to the mantle, "I always wanted a dog."

He shot her a pleading look but smiled when he caught her mischievous grin. He threw a tied flower bunch at her before he walked over to a trunk. After he had gathered a few things from it, Liz looked around the room. The floorboard had been replaced with a practiced hand. The chains were returned to the closet. Everything was as it was when she first burst into the cottage. There was an air of impatience in the room. He had been rocking on his heels, still draped in the old blanket; sheepishly, she turned her back so he could get dressed.

They walked out into a clear, sunny morning. Both squinted in the sunlight. Even in the daylight, the path to the cottage looked overgrown and little used. Liz noted the broken saplings where she had fallen the night before. Her Father picked up pieces of her tattered dress out of the bushes. She watched as he tucked them underneath his arm. She felt like she needed to say something, but words were lost to her. As they reached the hill behind the house, a small pile of ruined clothes lay strewn across the grass. This time, Liz picked them up. She smiled a little to herself as she walked past him and towards the comfort of their home.

"Next time, Father, we won't have to face our demons alone."

Her words stopped him; he stared at her back as she kept walking. His heart swelled as he watched his daughter with a new sense of awe, "Suppose not."

Memories

The granite was worn and smooth from weather and time. Most of the stone was covered in moss now. If it were not my name on the headstone, it would have been barely distinguishable from the rest of the stone. Not that it mattered anyway; it was written in a script that had long since fallen out of use. It might seem strange to sit on your gravesite, but after a century or two, it really was the only bit of my old life I had left. Today, however, it felt like I was coming home.

Home. What is that anyway?

It had been four decades since I was here last. Maybe three or four before that. Time loses its sting when it no longer matters. For me, it feels like I walk through time as if I were in a dream. I am never really aware anymore of it passing, other than it simply does. I just lost track of it. I am not even sure what brought me back this time. A longing? Nostalgia? No matter, here I am, once more, sitting on the top of my headstone, brushing off the fallen debris from the forest trees.

I recall when there was nothing here but the village graves. No trees, just open space and some flowering grasses. I remember the first trees. I think it was last century when I noticed the new saplings pushing through. That big oak over there is growing right through the metalsmith's grave. Actually, most of the gravesites are gone, and trees and other plant life have taken them over. No one even knows it is here. And why would they? This was just a small village from a long time ago. Everyone who called this place home has died, or their children moved away and forgot about this place. Yet, there was my stone, still just visible in the foliage. I just couldn't let mine disappear; I didn't know why, maybe because I had not gone, not really. I never actually died.

Leaning back against the stone, I felt the wet moss under my backside. The moisture seeped into my dress, but I didn't care. This was where my home was. These were the hills I ran through as a child. The valley just below was where the little houses stood around a small central square. It was that square, many centuries ago, where I left my normal farm life behind became..what? A Litch? A ghost? A spirit? What was

I exactly? I still don't really know. Even now, when I look at myself, my dark, almost smoky form of a body, and wonder.

Lifting my hand towards the sun, it remained a purplish black vapor but in a nearly solid form of a hand. I am solid enough to feel and be felt, yet at times, I was as tangible as mist. Twisting my hand over, I couldn't see my fingernails or any other fine detail. I was more of a semi-solid form of a woman in her early twenties. Even my hair moved in ghostly wisps about me. It, too, was the same purple-black as the rest of me. I wondered what my face looked like. You'd think one would remember her face, but I just can't. By some power, I lost my body, including all my features. I have a nose, eyes and a mouth, but it was smooth, dark, and hard to look at straight on, or so I had learned over time from others.

Interestingly, my eyes were still the same icy blue of my childhood. "Blue as the mountain lake," as my father would have said. I hadn't thought about my family in a long time. By some impulse, I felt the need to walk towards the valley. Maybe going down there would answer why I came there in the first place.

The valley itself hadn't changed much. Still the same rolling hills on either side, maybe less deep than from my childhood, but that could just be my imagination. I had not returned to the actual valley since the day I "died." The place where my village, my home, stood was just a large flat area that had faint ground tracinging in the grass of where the square once stood. I wondered if any traces of our houses still existed under the soil. Walking to the center, I felt the ground rise ever so slightly.

Once upon a time, this was a large mound built of stone and wood. In the center of that was a huge cut stone. Not sure who placed it there; it had always been there, according to everyone in the village. I recalled the strange loopy script on the stone. It was cleansed and washed every year at the spring festival. The unwed of age would take turns washing the stone and applying green paint to the cravings. It was a rite of passage, as well as a way to let everyone know that you were available to wed. I remember that people would come from all around, some would travel weeks to visit this stone. It was a source of great pride to house it in our little village.

Looking down at my feet, the round top of a gray stone poked out of the grass.

I wonder…

The ground was soft; digging my fingers into it, I dug a small portion away. The stone went down and began to widen. I couldn't say why, but I had to know. Was it still here?

Getting up quickly, I scanned the area for a stick or a stone, anything to help me dig deeper faster. I suppose I could have left and returned with a shovel, but that would have taken hours to get to the closest town, especially on foot. I just could not wait that long. Something inside was desperate to know if it was there. Just outside of the clearing I found a large stick that looked strong enough for the task. It was heavy, but I did not care. I don't need to uncover all of it, just enough to see that it was THE stone.

Digging, I felt my arms ache from the effort. I am not sure how long it took, just that morning had long passed, and the afternoon sun was beginning to dip towards the horizon. Wish I could say that sweat trickled down my brow from the effort, but I didn't sweat. It was funny the things you took for granted. I couldn't sweat, but I could ache. It never ceased to amaze me what I could and can not experience. Even after all this time, I still didn't fully understand my "condition."

At least my effort was not in vain. At my feet stood about three feet of the exposed rock. It was worn, but the layers of soil must have protected it from being too badly weathered. It had fared better than my headstone. The familiar scrolling script was still visible, though not as crisp as I recalled it from memory. My fingers trembled as I traced the patterns. Something deep inside me called to wash the stone once more and paint it in the green.

"Why not? Is it not spring? The festival would have happened about this time anyway."

My voice echoed off the empty hills. It startled me a little; I was used to being alone. I just didn't speak much out loud. I supposed the sound of my voice came as a bit of a surprise. With a renewed sense of purpose, I returned to the task of uncovering the stone. Gratefully, there was only about a foot left to uncover. It looked odd sitting in a pit. I didn't have anything to carry water to wash it. There was a stream closer to the gravesites. I felt myself walk to the stream, pulled the black cloak off my shoulders and dipped into the small stream. As I lifted it out of the frigid water, my thoughts rushed.

Why does this matter now?

With my cloak, I washed away the dirt and grime of centuries, still pondering the question of "why" in my mind. Without much effort, the process of gathering the herbs and clay to create the sacred paint came to me once more. A sweet melody filled the valley. It reminded me of the festival, with all of its color, music and smell of flowers. The music rang in my ears like I was there. It took me a moment to realize I was the one singing. The melody just kept pouring out, and my soul poured out with it. With each verse of the song, my fingers traced out the patterns of the ancient sacred script on the stone. As I traced over my past, my rite, I could faintly hear the village come alive around me.

All around me, the faces of my family and friends appeared. People I grew up with. Neighbors and people that came from afar. Old friends and family who lived in separate villages and towns embraced, smiled and made exchanges. Bright greens, yellows, reds, and pinks adorned everyone's clothing. The colors of spring, of life, after the long, dark and cold winters.

The maids with flowers and ribbons in their hair danced around the stone. The young men, eyes falling upon favorites, watched from the center as they used their tanned shirts to wash away the old flaking paint of the past year. Lively music played, filling the air with delight. Among them, I felt my feet move to the rhythm. A hand reached out for mine; instinctively, I grabbed it. When I did, my breath caught. My hand was a soft, fleshy pink. I had small brown freckles that made random patterns across the top. My fingernails were smooth, clean and still bitten down to the nubs. I used to hate how ugly my fingers looked. I felt myself marvel at having visible fingernails, bitten or not. The hand I held was a young man's; it was well-muscled and callused. His face was round with a firm set jaw, yet youthful, making him look more boyish than he was. I had seen him in past festivals. He was from one of the villages from the west, near the lakes. I recalled

my father mentioning once that he was the son of a
fisherman. Father liked the family. I wondered if he
may have encouraged the encounter. Not that I
minded. He was nice to look at and had a strong grip.
He spoke little, but I knew I could live with that. We
dance around the mound with wild abandon. His hand
never left mine.

The music changed. It was the signal for the girls
who hoped to wed to gather and sing while they
painted the sacred stone. Our song was to ask the god
of Death to retreat for a time while we entice the god
of Life to return. The paint was made from the herbs
that were the first life to sprout up through the snow,
mixed with clay that represented the earth we all
would become once we died. Once we all took a turn
tracing the carvings on the stone, the maidens would
all turn to the men who had gathered around and
waited to have a token placed into her hand by the wise
woman who represented an interested party.

Each token had a match. Each girl was to walk
down and show her father or male head of the family
her token, and he would seek out the match to discuss
if an arrangement was to be made or not. Sometimes,

girls were given a closed flower bud. This meant that they were not yet ready to be wed. I stood with the rest, my heart hopeful to match the token of the fisherman's son. He seemed as good a match as any; at least he was attractive and had a nice livelihood ahead of him.

The village-wise woman walked around our circle, placing the token into our hands. Only she knew which token to give exactly. It felt like time had slowed to a snail's pace. The desire to peek into your hand was strong, but everyone knew that if you peeked before the ritual was over, it would bring misfortune to the future of the young lady. All of us said we believed it was true, but I often wondered if bad fortune really followed if you peeked. I couldn't stop myself; my fingers peeled away from the token in my palm ever so slightly. As casually as possible, I glanced down. I caught a glimpse of a shiny, dark object. It felt smooth, round, and somewhat heavy.

A stone? What an odd token.

I tightened my fingers around the object. It felt oddly cold for being in my hand this long. Lost in my thoughts, I nearly missed our cue to leave our circle on the mound and return to our families. As I began to step away, for just a moment, I turned around to look at the stone. The green paint appeared to be glowing, with a dark, ghostly hand tracing out the patterns. It looked like a window to another place; the stone was there, but instead of my village, there was just openness. It looked different, too, lower, like at ground level. A dark figure of a young woman shaped like my shadow placed her head against the stone. In a flash, the vision was gone, and the stone was on the mound surrounded by the village once more.

Too much wine.

I ignored the unsettled feeling in my gut and joined my family. In moments, I would discover my fate.

Silence.

I opened my eyes, unaware I had closed them. My hand and head rested on the stone, and what?

Was this warmth running down my cheeks?

Tears? Strange.

I had not cried in so long; I didn't think I still could. I relived that day and, at the same time, somehow, saw myself there and then and the here and now all at once.

Like a window between the two points. Emotions, thoughts, and regrets that I had tucked away for a century awakened within me.

I should not have looked.

How often did that thought burn inside my mind? How often did I abuse myself for what misfortune I placed upon my family with my actions that night? My hand clenched in fury as I pounded on the stone. The scream from my throat was wild, loud and long. It was Primal. I didn't care. I kept pounding the stone, screaming and crying until all the light in the valley had gone. I felt weary drained, and like a heavy weight had finally been lifted. I had carried that rage for far too long. I sat in my pit with my back up against the stone and just listened to the silence around me. My mind was still asking why it all happened. The stone felt warm compared to the growing chill in the air. I should not have cared; the elements had no harmful effect on me. However, I still felt them. The warmth was inviting. I let it and my weariness take me into the dark oblivion of sleep.

Ina. Ina Allure. "Ina Allure".

The voice was soft but powerful. A male voice that I both heard and felt in my mind with a disorientating effect that I wasn't sure if it was my imagination or not. I swore that someone had called my name, my full birth name. Sitting up slowly, I looked around. It was dark, and I guessed it to be late into the evening. My eyes saw well in darkness, a perk of my current state, I suppose. The valley was as empty as it was before, except the feeling of a presence. A very powerful presence.

"Who's there?" I quietly asked the darkness.

"Look at your feet, Ina." *You returned. I have been waiting; you are finally ready.*

The male voice commanded, yet was still gentle. Who or whatever *he* had spoken aloud and in my mind simultaneously. It was not hard to understand, but the experience was somewhat dizzying.

"Who are you, and how do you know me?"

My voice was hoarse from earlier. I continued to scan the area. He sounded as if he was next to me. All I saw was the valley and the stone. Yet, I could tell there was a presence behind me, at my shoulder.

Look down, Ina.

My eyes traveled the length of my own body to my feet. On the ground, directly at my toes, sat something round and dark.

"That is impossible," I whispered to myself.

"Is it?" The voice was no more than a whisper itself. I could feel the warmth of his breath across my cheek and over my ear. If I still had blood, it would have run cold. I turned to confront him. Nothing. There was nothing there. I spun around, searching; I was the only being as far as the eye could see. With deliberate caution, I stooped down and tightly clutched the item. It felt smooth and cool, with a familiar weight to it.

Just like that night, I recalled.

Look in your hand, Ina.

No. I won't make that mistake again.

They are not here, Ina. They are all gone. It is just us here now.

I am afraid.

"You don't have to be. But please, don't turn around yet. Just look at it, and remember," the voice spoke quietly, almost pleadingly.

I had to will myself to obey. Every one of my being wanted to turn around to see who was there. Within me, a war had erupted, something about him, his voice, that caused me to be afraid and comforted all at once. I wanted to run away. I wanted to stay. I wanted to disappear from this unknown presence, but I needed to know. Somehow, I knew that for the first time in centuries, I would get answers tonight.

Yes, you will, the voice confirmed.

"How did you-"

It is part of who I am. I know what lies in your heart. Do not fear Ina. Just look one last time.

I drew in a breath and opened my hand. Once more, I was transported back in time, back to the festival. Once more I was both my past self living in the moment and a mute invisible spectator watching myself experiencing the memory.

I was in our small wooden home. It was barely more than a hut, just a small square held together with sticks, stones and mud. Thatch covered the timbers above, and furs covered the walls. In the center was the fire, still lit. A white tendril of smoke snaked up through the small hole in the center of the roofing. The hut felt warm from the day's activities mixed with that comforting familiarity of home. I stood before my father, my hand still closed. He offered his hand, turning it over to reveal a silver pendant in the shape of a fish. My heart sank. I knew it did not match my token. The fisherman's son had requested my hand from my father, but the wise woman had placed something different in my hand. My parents noticed the disappointment on my face. My mother whispered urgently into my father's ear.

They knew I peeked. I began to panic. *They know I will be cursed with misfortune for myself and for the whole family.*

But before anyone said anything to me, the wise woman rushed into our hut. Shouting something at me and my family. With her sudden appearance and flurry of words, my mind had gone numb, and I did not understand anything that was said. Her words pushed my parents into desperate action, pulling my hand open with confusion and arguing with the wise woman about protection talismans. In the chaos, my black, smooth stone dropped to the ground. We all just stared at it like a venomous snake that had gotten loose.

Its surface was so polished it reflected our faces at us. I saw horror in all but my face. My face held confusion that transformed into wonder and finally into hard-set determination. I bent over and picked up the stone, only to have the wise woman slap it out of my hand. For some reason, this angered me. It was mine. It was intended for me and me alone. She was the one that placed it there in the first place, so why is she so angry at me? So what if I looked? I was disappointed at first that it did not match, but now, who was this mystery person who sought my hand but had not spoken first with my father? Was there someone who was able to outwit the wise woman and get her to place the stone in my hand? Who was this person that caused such fear in my family and the wise woman? Tears of frustration stung my eyes. I pushed the woman away and grabbed the stone from the ground, then ran out the door. This was supposed to be my night, my year, and it is crashing down around me.

I heard them shouting my name from behind, but I would not go back. I had to know. To return to the mound and stand upon it alone during the spring festival was said to invoke the anger of the god of Life and prolong the winter, but I didn't care. I knew that I was now destined for misfortune, so what did matter?

I looked around at the crowd, and somehow, everything seemed wrong. The bright colors became garish, and the people's joy felt like a mockery. I raced up, tearing away from hands that pulled at me, ignoring the shouts and pleas. I reached the stone on the mound, gripping my token and raised it above my head. The lights of the fires and torches reflected off its dark surface. A sudden stillness swept across the crowd.

Silence. That horrible silence.

All around me, the festival had come to an abrupt halt. Even the music died. From the direction of my home, the crowd parted, and the wise woman stepped forward. Her face looked angry, or maybe it was sad. Tears still rolled down my cheeks. I did not understand.

What is happening? My mind screamed over and over.

"Curse upon you," she spat at me while pointing.

My parents stood with tears in their eyes. My mother turned her face away from me. My father put his arm around her shoulders and shook his head as he held her. The shame in his eyes crushed me like a bug under my heel. Every eye was on me. My heart dropped to my stomach. I dropped to my knees, knowing what was coming next. One by one, the word passed over each person's lips, "Cursed".

The rites that night would not finish for me. All the other girls would continue with finding their match or be told to wait another year. Feasting would happen, and the couples would return after midnight here to this mound, hand in hand, and trace the green lines over with a drop of each of their blood. It was an offering to the god of Death to bind their lives together as a couple and, at the same time, a promise to the god of Life of a new life to begin. To be there alone and then cursed on top of that meant I could ruin the lives of all those who were to finish the rite that night.

I waited. I knew that being a curse upon the mound required me to offer sacrifice to cleanse it. I still did not understand why this black stone caused such a reaction from everyone. I fought with tears while I told everyone I was sorry for looking and pleading to explain why I was now marked as cursed. The stone rolled from my hands down the mound and into the crowd. The wise woman picked it up with a cloth, lifting it towards me. I could see the outline of myself in it, a shadowy, wispy version of myself without features. My shadow reflection looked as if she danced, a movement I attributed to the firelight. It ignited this deep desire to be her, to be free like her. That reflection was something unearthly to me. A growing sense of being something more than a fisherman's wife had begun to take root in my soul. She was beautiful, and I wanted to be her.

"How did you get this stone Ina?" her voice cracked, "Your token I placed in your hand matched your father's. "

"I peeked," I whispered.

"Lies. I placed the correct token in your hand," she waved my stone in front of the crowd for all to see, her voice raised to be heard over the murmurings of the growing crowd.

"This belongs in the temple of the god of Death. Did you take it before the festival?"

My head shot up, anger growing hot inside of me.

A god stone? I would never… She thinks I stole that stone! Do they all think I stole that stone?!!

"I have never seen that stone before in my life! I didn't even know it was there!" My voice rose to a shout, "You all think me a thief?! And of gods, no less! Do you not know me? Do you all think that little of me?!" Rage continued to boil inside me. With an energy I didn't know I had, I lept of the mound onto the old woman, my eyes on the stone. I am sure I had hurt her when I landed on her, but I didn't care anymore. I tore the stone from her hands, lifting it up to the sky shouting, "I am innocent! But, if you all believe me a thief and cursed, then so be it! A curse on all of you! This token is rightfully mine, and no one is taking it from me."

The next thing I knew, I was running away. Away from the village, from the people, from the light, from everything. I ran until I reached the woods in the hills where the dead slept. I turned to see the commotion below. I checked to see if the stone was still in my hand. With relief, it still sat cool and heavy in my palm. No reflection now, but I knew I had to leave, if for no other reason than just to get my thoughts together. I turned back around and walked forward. No plan on where I was going to go, just away. Away into darkness.

It seemed like a dream the way the village disappeared behind me; even the night seemed to stand still. All sounds had faded away. Just the sound of the crunching of leaves and overwintered growth underfoot filled the void. In front of me, the hill dropped off to a craggy ravine. Somehow, I was on the other side of the valley. I didn't feel like I walked that far, but the edge of the world, as I knew it, was there in front of me. Above, the moon had dipped towards the hill; it would be morning soon. Had I numbly walked all night long?

The ravine was dangerous, especially in the dark. I felt something in me just snap. My thoughts whirled in my head. My life, my dreams, all I had known rushed past me like a swollen river. I took another step forward. Finally, my thoughts swirled around one thought; I would not live a life where it shamed me and my family. I didn't know how the stone came to be my token, but I knew I had to offer a sacrifice to make things right. Without a second thought, I lept, clutching the cool stone to my chest, my only possession now.

The rushing feel of the land peeling away from me was like having a blanket being pulled off a warm bed.

The air felt crisp against my skin.

Floating, falling.

This will be freedom.

Time slowed.

The sacrifice would be met.

Silence.

I knew I was going to hit the ground and break my neck, or at least I hoped it would be quick like that. I let my mind go, waiting for the impact.

Nothing.

There was nothing. I blinked my eyes a few times. All around me was darkness, stillness, and nothingness.

The Stone!

I feared that I had dropped it in my fall. The stone was all that mattered, and I needed it. I don't know why I did, but I just felt a strong sense of need for it, even if it didn't matter once I hit the bottom. I struggled to maneuver myself to look and see.

Was I still falling? Was already dead? I couldn't tell.

I felt strange, weightless. I looked at my hands for my stone; it was indeed gone, but my hands! Oh, my gods! My hands! My hands had disappeared, too. In their place was a dark shadow of themselves. My arms, as well. I was not falling anymore, either. I was standing at the bottom of the ravine. The shock of my situation caused me to look around dumbly. I felt my world sway from one side then to another.

The next thing I remembered, I found myself laying in a small trickle of water at the bottom of a ravine, but not the one I jumped into. This one was somewhere far warmer than anything I had experienced before, and drier too. I could just make out strange small shrubs and trees that were bare of leaves, and both had sharp-looking spines instead. In the pale morning light, I could just make myself out. Beyond anything that made any sense, my body was whole, naked, and very much still alive. However, I was also very much changed. My entire body was as dark and as featureless as the stone had been. Panic set in. My voiceless scream into the morning light was lost to the dawn.

A flash of blinding light brought me back. I blinked. I was once more standing in the pit next to the ritual stone in the dark. In my hand, the cool, beautiful stone sat. The moonlight was enough to see my shadowy reflection, that same reflection from so long ago. I felt the beginning of comprehension blossoming in my heart, but it felt fragile. I did not turn around, not wanting to take the risk of what might happen.

"You saved me and changed me that night," I whispered.

"Yes."

"I have always been this reflection."

"You are finally beginning to see," his voice sounded more excited as if he had been longing for me to make the connection. My heart began to pound harder; I could feel a flush my cheeks if it were even possible.

"Why?"

The voice did not respond right away. It felt as though he was thinking. I waited. I continued to resist the urge to turn around. A part of me was afraid actually to see.

"Do you still not know?" He sounded amused.

Looking at the black stone, I knew, yet still was unsure of my feelings.

"You, you changed the fish token to your stone. You gave me your god stone. I still don't understand why."

Are you afraid? The voice softly resonated through my whole soul.

Yes.

There was never a reason to be Ina. I chose you. And I have waited for you.

I sensed a shifting in his presence like he was moving his weight from one side to another. I felt that fiery passion of excitement reverberates through me. I felt it during that spring festival before I peeked at the token. It was a mix of not knowing if I'd be chosen and wondering how my future would be fated that night. Fear was still mixed in, that fear of the unknown. I felt it deep inside me. The longing that brought me here. The reason I kept coming back, but never to the mound. This time, I came back home to finish what was started so many centuries ago finally.

"You chose me" I cleared my throat, nervous to voice the rest,"you chose me to be."

"Yes. I chose you, Ina, to be mine." He finished. His voice sounded more solid than before.

Turn around Ina Allure and see.

I closed my eyes and turned. I felt a solid hand gently brush my cheek. His touch sent an electric shock of hope down my spine. I opened my eyes. Before me was the tall, dark, shadowy form of a man;

his form waived from solid to misty, much like my own. His eyes were also blue, but his held a depth that was like the endless expanse of the sky, and held a gentleness I would not have fathomed possible. I knew him. I had brushed past him so many times it was like greeting an old friend. Before me, I beheld the god of Death.

He held his hand, turned it over and in his palm rested a stone identical to my own. When I looked down, my face reflected at me. I was surprised that my features had become sharper and more distinct. Looking up at his face, he, too, had become more defined. His squared jaw was commanding, as was the rest of his face, but it was a kind face. He smiled warmly. With a girlish excitement, I gazed into a very handsome man.

"Consider it a gift. It is the least I can do after all this time." His eyes shied away from my gaze a little as I ran my free hand over my face. He cleared his throat, causing me to pause from touching my face. Still not looking directly at me, put his hand out towards me as he offered me his token. I could feel the heat rising once more up my neck, through my cheeks and into my ears. For centuries, I had wondered what this moment would be like if I had not peeked, but instead, a fisherman's son, in front of me, was the god of Death. The fear I had had melted away; in its place was heightened anticipation. A part of me told me that I should be very afraid that I was standing face-to-face with Death, but I only felt excitement. He stood tall and formally and looked at me intently.

"Ina Allure of the valley," his voice was almost nervously boyish, "Do you choose me?"

Without the ability to use my words I took my free hand, placed it over his token, placing my own in his other hand. As our hands clasped over each other, the stones began to warm. I felt a tension release from his body. I couldn't help but giggle a little. He looked at me questioningly.

"I would have not thought that a god could be nervous."

"I was concerned you would refuse my offer wIth what I did and how I had to change you. I know that this was not what you pictured. I…I am not very well versed in the matters of the living or of the heart.

Looking back, I probably could have approached it differently, and you would not have had to deal with all that happened."

I know you have so many questions. There will be answers. But for tonight, let them rest. I am sorry I didn't finish what I started then. Let me do so now.

I nodded, lifted his hand to my lips and kissed the top. He felt warm and inviting; I felt like every part of me wanted to be close to him. I knew now that nothing that had happened mattered anymore; I was where I desired to be, and I wanted to be his more than anything. I moved his stone to my other hand, holding both of them tightly together, signifying that I had fully accepted his terms. He looked up to the moon.

Midnight, my dear Ina.

With his other hand, he produced a small dagger seemingly from nowhere and pricked his finger. No crimson blood fell from his hand; only a dark, wispy mist ran down his hand like a rolling black fog. He repeated the motion with my hand, and I, too, did not bleed red lifeblood but an onyx ichor that was not quite fluid. I looked up to his face, and he smiled at me with adoration I had never seen before. Without fear, I pressed my hand into his, letting our essence flow from one hand to the other. It caused a tingling sensation down my arm. We traced the lines on the stone with our interlocked hands; the green paint flaked away as we did. In its place, a trickle of black remained. It looked smoky and ready to lift away at any moment but never did.

The ritual was complete. What was started was finally finished. The god of Death smiled at me; he pulled me close. In my mind, I could hear faint music playing. His head against mine, he led me into a gentle sway to that distance melody. Under the slowly lighting sky, he whispered into my ear the sweet song:

Flutter and flight, the memories of the Night
Like the moth to the light.
No escape from their wings,
Our Fate they do bring.

I leaned into his chest, picking up the song with a voice I thought I had lost:

O God of Death, bind our blood we offer,
Bind us here and in the thereafter.

God of Life, light our path anew,
We are now one who were once two.

The pale colors of lavender and gold began to fill the horizon. As the dawn began to break, he pulled me in close. His lips cut my song off as he placed them firmly against my own. For a brief moment, I was unsure what to do. As quickly as my shock from his kiss came, it left. I pulled him closer to me and I kissed him harder; our stones dropped to the foot of the ritual stone as I did. As I felt my old self finally die, I sang the last stanza of the wedding song in my mind:

Let the memories of the past die,
In this moment, let our hearts fly.
With our past now gone,
Our new life has begun.

As the rays of dawn hit our backs, our bodies began to fade, but I was not afraid. The god of Death looked down and smiled. I was going home.

www.ingramcontent.com/pod-product-compliance
Lightning Source LLC
Chambersburg PA
CBHW021559310726
48972CB00003B/870